S0-DZC-740

DIGITAL
DIGIMON
MONSTERS
™

J. E. Bright

RETURN TO
INFINITY
MOUNTAIN

HarperEntertainment
An Imprint of HarperCollins*Publishers*
10 East 53rd Street, New York, NY 10022

HarperCollins books are available at special quantity discounts for bulk purchases for sales
promotions, premiums, or fund-raising. For information please call or write:
Special Markets Department, HarperCollins Publishers Inc., 10 East 53rd Street, New York, NY 10022.
Telephone: (212) 207-7528. Fax: (212) 207-7222.

ISBN 0-06-107196-X

First printing: November 2000

Printed in the United States of America

Visit HarperEntertainment on the World Wide Web at www.harpercollins.com

Seven kids were mysteriously transported to a strange island in the middle of DigiWorld. After exploring all over File Island looking for a way to get home, the seven kids climbed Infinity Mountain with their Digimon friends.

At the foot of this fantastically high mountain, Tai Kamiya, Matt Ishida, Sora Takenouchi, Izzy Izumi, T.K. Takaishi, Mimi Tachikawa, and Joe Kido found a white mansion. Inside, they discovered a welcoming feast fit for royalty. They ate until they were stuffed, bathed in the mansion's hot tubs, and then went to sleep in the comfy beds.

That night, the most evil Digimon of all showed up— Devimon! The mansion was merely an illusion created by Devimon as a trap! The food they'd eaten wasn't even real!

With a flap of his gray tattered wings, Devimon's red eyes glowed. He smiled, showing his pointy fangs. Then he cast a spell that set off an enormous earthquake— rupturing File Island into floating parts!

Worst of all, before the kids could even get out of bed, Devimon had scattered them to faraway chunks of the broken island. They were totally separated from each other!

"Now that they're on their own," Devimon bellowed, "those little intruders will meet their doom!" He raised his wings and hundreds of his evil Black Gears soared up behind him. "Now fly!" he shouted.

Then Devimon's chilling laugh rang out across the broken parts of File Island.

Part

1

ADVENTURE IN FREEZELAND

Tai held on to the bed as it plummeted through the air.

He was high in the sky, dressed only in his underpants and sneakers.

Agumon clung desperately to the bed-covers next to him. They had been falling like stones ever since Devimon had hurled them from File Island.

"Tai, it's cold," Agumon cried. He looked like a minia-ture dinosaur. "I'm hungry, and you can't find your clothes. I just wish we were on solid ground!"

They plunged through a cloudbank, and the bed fell toward a huge iceberg bobbing in an ocean of frigid blue water.

"Next time be careful what you wish for!" Tai shouted. "You just might get it!"

The bed slammed into the iceberg with a solid crunch. Tai and Agumon were thrown clear. Screaming, they landed face-first in the thick snow.

Tai surfaced next to Agumon with a gasp. Tai's lips were blue, and his teeth chattered. Then he saw that Agumon's head was stuck in the snow. The Digimon waggled his lizard-like legs.

"Hey!" Agumon hollered, his voice muffled. "Who turned out the lights?"

"Take it easy," Tai called as he grabbed Agumon's legs.

"I'll pull you out!" With a yank, Agumon popped free, and Tai fell backward. Frozen clothes landed on Tai's chest.

"Hey, look," Tai said. He scrambled to his feet and held

out his shirt encased in ice. "I found my clothes. Except they're too cool even for me now!"

"Don't worry," Agumon replied. "I can give you the latest hot look."

Agumon puffed a fireball out of his mouth, which defrosted Tai's shirt in a cloud of hissing steam.

Tai grinned. "Hey, Agumon, that's smoking!" he cheered. "Now can you hook up my pants?" He held up his shorts.

Agumon let out another spurt of his Pepper Breath.

But this time, Tai's shorts caught on fire!

Tai waved out the flames, but his pants were left charred and smoky.

"Oops," Agumon said sheepishly. "I nuked them a little too long. But you won't be cold anymore!"

Tai rolled his eyes and put on his crispy outfit. He slipped his goggles onto his forehead to hold back his wild hair, and peered around the snowy area where they'd crash-landed. He and Agumon were standing near a jagged wall of ice that glittered in the sunlight like blue crystal.

Nearby was a row of old-fashioned mailboxes mounted on poles.

"Mailboxes!" Tai exclaimed. "I wish we could mail our-

selves home, but I doubt anybody bothers to pick up the mail here!"

Tai pulled out his mini-spyglass to peer over the ocean.

Far across the water, he spotted the top of Infinity Mountain poking up through a cloud. Other islands and icebergs floated in the distance.

"It looks like the only way we'll ever leave Freezeland is to take a long, cold swim," Tai said with a sigh. "If the mountain is drifting farther away, then our friends are, too. They must be out there on those other islands."

Agumon nodded. "I guess it could be worse," he said. "There could be evil Digimon attacking us. It's too quiet here."

The quiet only lasted another second, broken by a strange creaking sound. Then the ice in front of Agumon split open at his feet. Snow exploded upward, spewing out of a jagged crack.

Tai and Agumon screamed as a giant creature leaped out of the icy chasm.

"Frigimon!" the creature hollered. He was a huge white snowman with a plump body and big coal-black eyes. Two red buttons shone on his chest.

"I've heard of him!" Agumon cried. "But he's a gentle Digimon!"

Frigimon wound up his arm, preparing to hurl something.

"Don't look now," Tai shouted, "but he's about to *gently* squash us flat!"

Frigimon flung a gigantic snowball. Tai and Agumon leaped out of the way, tumbling down a slippery hill. They slid past Frigimon, gliding on their stomachs.

"Oh, great!" Agumon yelled. "My belly's freezing!" He glanced up at the snowman and gasped when he saw what was sticking out of Frigimon's back. "It's a Black Gear!"

Frigimon wound up for another attack. "Subzero Ice Punch!" he bellowed. He swung his fist, but Tai and Agumon ducked, and Frigimon missed Tai's head. His fist clobbered a mailbox, which was instantly coated in ice.

"I guess I better heat things up!" Agumon declared. He bravely faced the Gear-infected Digimon and spat a puff of fire.

The burst of Pepper Breath soared toward Frigimon, but the snowman's fists smashed it apart easily.

"I assume you have a backup plan?" Tai asked.

"Yes," Agumon replied. "Run!"

Frigimon chased them as they fled through the snow. The snowman's every step shook the iceberg, and he quickly caught up to Tai and Agumon.

He tried to bash them with another punch, but the snowman missed as Tai turned sharply. Frigimon twirled from the force of his punch before he recovered.

"Come back here and fight Frigimon!" the snowman growled.

Putting on an extra burst of speed, Tai and Agumon

gained a small lead. They ducked through a passage in the ice wall, panting.

But past the short passage was a cliff of frozen rock—a dead end!

"Uh-oh," Agumon said. He skidded to a stop, groaning when he saw Frigimon behind them.

"Going somewhere?" Frigimon asked.

"We're trapped like ice mice!" Tai cried. "There's nowhere else to run!"

Frigimon's eyes glinted with menace as he backed Tai and Agumon up against the curved wall of the icy cliff.

"I've got an idea!" Agumon hissed to Tai. "Pick me up and throw me at him! If I can land on his back, I can vaporize that Black Gear with my Pepper Breath!"

Tai grabbed Agumon around the waist and hoisted him off the ground. "I don't know if this is going to work, dude," Tai said with a grunt. "I can barely lift you, much less throw you, *Tubbymon*!"

With a holler, Frigimon charged. He raised his arm for a crushing blow. "Subzero Ice Punch!" Frigimon bellowed.

Squealing in terror, Tai and Agumon threw themselves against the snow, and they slipped between Frigimon's stumpy legs. Frigimon couldn't stop running in time, and his punch slammed into the ice wall. With a horribly loud

14

crash, an avalanche tumbled down, burying Frigimon in ice chunks.

Tai and Agumon scrambled to their feet. "Okay, now's our shot," Tai told his little Digimon friend. "Roll up into a ball, son!"

Agumon curled up into a neat circle, with his head between his knobby knees. "You mean like this?" he asked, covering his head with his claws.

"Yep," Tai replied. "Now I'll show you why I'm my soccer team's best striker!"

Just as Frigimon burst out of the snow pile with a colossal roar, Tai gave Agumon a solid kick.

Still curled, Agumon sailed at Frigimon. As he whizzed over the monster, Agumon unfolded, twisting in the air. He grabbed onto Frigimon's back—next to the Black Gear!

Without wasting a second, Agumon let loose a blast of his Pepper Breath. The fireball struck the Black Gear, and Frigimon freaked out.

Screaming in pain, Frigimon bucked wildly, throwing Agumon off him. The Black Gear fell into the snow. It disintegrated in a sizzle of evil. Frigimon collapsed like a falling mattress, face down.

"Yahoo!" Agumon yelled. "We did it!"

Slowly, Frigimon climbed to his knees. All the evil had left his coal eyes. "What am I doing laying here?" he asked in a silly, friendly voice.

"A Black Gear was on you," Agumon replied, "and you almost turned us into ice sculptures!"

"Ooh, I'm so sorry," Frigimon said. He smiled and his eyes twinkled merrily. "Thank you for destroying the Gear. I'm glad you're both all right."

"Have you seen some more kids like me?" Tai asked the snowman.

Frigimon raised his fist up to his mouth and tapped his

lips. "Hmm," he said, "come to think of it, I *did* see another boy like you. He was with a Gabumon." Frigimon pointed over the ocean where another iceberg was bobbing. "They fell onto that other island over there."

"You saw Gabumon!" Agumon cheered.

"And Matt!" Tai added. His voice sounded excited, but then it dropped to a sad whisper. "Perfect," he muttered. "Matt *would* land that far away. It's too cold to swim, and we're drifting at one hundred miles a year!"

Frigimon climbed to his feet. "You're a weird kid," he

told Tai, "but since you got that Black Gear out of my aching back, I'll help you get across." Frigimon hustled to the frozen shore, and slammed his fist down on the water. "Subzero Ice Punch!" he shouted.

Instantly, a thick path of ice froze outward from Frigimon's punch, creating a solid walkway a dozen feet into the ocean.

Tai, Agumon, and Frigimon hurried to the end of the frozen path. Tai peered across the vast body of icy water.

It was a long, *long* way to the next island.

After a few hours of marching across the frozen strip of ocean, Tai and Agumon were getting exhausted. They dawdled behind the big snowman.

"Man, that island's just as far away as ever!" Tai grumbled. His legs wobbled, so he plopped down to sit on the bridge. "Let's take five, you guys," he said, "then we'll boogie on." Tai shivered with cold, even though he was sweating from their long walk.

Agumon slumped down next to Tai, pooped.

"The island's still moving," Frigimon warned. "If we stop, we may not be able to catch up."

"Agumon," Tai joked, "if you could fly like Birdramon, we'd be there already!"

"Well, I can't," Agumon replied, annoyed. He crossed his arms and turned away with his snout in the air.

Tai stood up and peered over Agumon's shoulder. "Birdramon probably couldn't fly in the cold, anyway," he

said with a chuckle. "No one can toast my clothes like you," he added. "C'mon, laugh!"

Agumon closed his eyes. "No way," he said, pouting.

Frigimon grabbed Tai and Agumon in each of his huge hands.

"I hate to see friends fight," he said. "I'll carry you both across." Frigimon raised them to his shoulders, and they settled back against his chest. "There, nice and comfy?"

"Yeah," Tai answered, "comfy as a mackerel on ice! But at least we'll still be nice and fresh when we get there!"

Frigimon strolled down the ice bridge. "Did I ever tell you about the party I went to that the Numemons crashed?" he asked. The Numemons were gross Digimon that lived in the sewers. "Now *that's* a party no one will forget!"

Matt was lost in a blizzard. Flurries pelted him as he stumbled through the thick snow. Matt was freezing in his olive green T-shirt, but he couldn't give up his search for his little brother. "T.K.!" he screamed into the howling, icy wind. "T.K., can you hear me?"

As Matt staggered through an evergreen forest, he began to cough. "Where are you, T.K.?" he moaned. Then he collapsed face-first into the snow.

A few minutes passed before Gabumon caught up to Matt. "Matt!" Gabumon cried when he saw his fallen friend. "Oh!"

Gabumon had a fuzzy hamster body, with zebra stripes down to his chunky lizard legs and tail. He rushed over to Matt's side. "You must save your strength!" he scolded.

Matt pushed himself off the cold ground with his arms. But he coughed again, and collapsed, wheezing pitifully.

"Look, there's a cave!" Gabumon said. He pointed to a dark hole in a boulder nearby. "Let's go in and get warm, until the storm's over."

Matt suddenly jumped to his feet. "A cave!" he shouted. "Of course, *that's* where T.K. is! Yes!" Matt charged into the dark hole, screaming, "T.K.!"

Inside, Matt gasped in disappointment as he pulled up to a short stop. The cave was empty. "I was so sure he'd be here!" he cried, slumping dejectedly.

Gabumon gathered a bunch of twigs, and puffed on them with his blue fire breath. A cheerful blaze was soon crackling. "There, now," Gabumon said. "Come and sit by the fire."

When Matt didn't move, Gabumon sighed. "Matt," he said patiently, "you can't help T.K.—or anybody for that matter—if you get sick. You must rest, to stay strong."

"No!" Matt wailed. "I've got to go back out there and find him! I feel fi—" His words were cut off by a bout of coughing.

Gabumon gently steered Matt toward the flickering campfire. "Sit down," Gabumon said. "You stay in the cave . . . *I'll* go and look for T.K."

"Huh?" Matt murmured, amazed.

"Hey, come on!" Gabumon replied. "I'm your Digimon, remember? I'm here to help you, whether it's hot or cold." Then Gabumon laughed. "Besides, I've got a built-in warm fur coat, which you haven't!"

As soon as Matt had settled by the fire, Gabumon strode to the cave's exit. "I'll be back in two shakes of a Digitail!" he called, disappearing into the blizzard.

Matt stared into the flames, coughing softly. "Poor little T.K.," he whispered. "It's just not right. He's *my* little brother . . . I should be the one out looking for him!"

"T.K.!" Matt bawled.

Then he rushed out of the cave and vanished into the falling snow.

A few hours later, Gabumon hurried back toward the cave, exhausted from his search. "Well, no sign of T.K. out here anywhere," Gabumon said sadly. "Matt'll be really disappointed."

Up ahead, Gabumon spotted a hole in the snow—in the shape of a boy! "Matt!" he gasped.

Gabumon hurried over to check out Matt. He was facedown . . . and he wasn't moving! "What're you doing?" Gabumon asked as he grabbed Matt's hands. His friend didn't move or answer. "I told you not to leave! Matt, can you hear me?"

Gabumon dragged Matt toward the cave. He found the shelter quickly, and pulled his friend to the fire. Gabumon built a soft bed of leaves, and rested Matt on it.

"He's frozen," Gabumon said nervously. "I've got to warm him up or else . . . or else he'll never make it. How else can I keep him warm? All I have is my own fur, and—hey, that's it!"

Stepping closer to the fire, Gabumon slipped out of his fur. "Why not?" he told himself. "No one's here to see me."

When he had stripped, Gabumon giggled. "Naked Digimon!" he chirped. Then he smoothed the thick fur down over Matt. "Here you go, my friend."

Gabumon snuggled close to keep Matt even warmer. "You'll feel better in no time," he whispered as he dropped off to sleep. "Good thing we're alone here."

Outside, the blizzard still raged.

And a mysterious, hulking figure peered at the cave from his hiding spot in the evergreen trees.

Early the next morning, Frigimon reached the end of the ice bridge and stepped onto a new island. Behind him, the sunrise was dazzling against the shimmering water. "Hey, you two, we're here!"

Tai and Agumon woke high in Frigimon's arms, and quickly hopped down. "Yahoo!" Tai exclaimed, pulling out his spyglass. He peered at the groves of pine trees around the shoreline. "But where did Gabumon and Matt land?"

Frigimon pointed at a cliff where more evergreens grew. "They must be up there somewhere, in that forest," he replied.

Tai rolled his eyes. "Sure, let's go for a hike," he said as they began to climb up a snowy slope. "Then after that we'll hike, and then we can hike some more! Sheesh!"

"Hey!" Agumon said, pointing. "Look!" Sticking out of the edge of the forest was a four-poster bed. It leaned sideways against a tree trunk as though it had crashed there.

"Matt must be around here somewhere!" Tai exclaimed. He cupped his hands around his mouth. "Matt! Matt, can you hear me?"

In the cave, Matt woke with a jolt. As he opened his eyes, Gabumon snatched up his fur and hurried behind a rock.

"Huh?" Matt murmured. "Gabumon! You . . . you took your fur off for—" Matt blushed. "Uh . . . well, *thanks*."

Fully dressed, Gabumon stepped out from behind the rock. "Uh . . . good to see you're up and feeling—" Gabumon sneezed three times. "Better!"

"You kept me warm and now you have my cold," Matt said. "I'll bet you looked pretty funny with no fur on, Gabumon!" He laughed. "Thank you."

"It's okay," Gabumon replied cheerfully.

"Matt!" a voice called from outside. "Gabumon!"

Matt gasped and jumped to his feet.

"It's Tai and Agumon!" Gabumon exclaimed. "They're here—" Gabumon let out another sneeze.

"Matt!" Tai called again.

Matt rushed out of the cave. "Tai!" he shouted. When they met, Tai and Matt gave each other a high-five.

Agumon grabbed Gabumon in a hug.

Tai laughed happily. "I thought we'd never find you

guys! It's a good thing we met up with Frigimon!" He nodded his head toward the giant Digimon waiting behind
him. "He happened to see you two fall on this island and
then he got us here in no time!"

Frigimon smiled. "Subzero Ice Punch, you know," he
said modestly.

"Did you see anyone else?" Matt asked the snowman.

"No," Frigimon replied. "When it rains kids, I usually
notice. You were the only two who fell here. If there are
more of you, they must be on the other islands."

Matt hung his head. "Poor T.K.," he whispered.

Gabumon sneezed again—almost nailing Agumon with
the gross spray!

"Hey, watch it, dude!" Agumon warned.

"Sorry," Gabumon said. "I'm not used to having a cold!"

Frigimon rubbed his hand against his chin. "A cold, eh?" he muttered. "I have an idea . . ." Without even saying good-bye, he strode off into the forest.

"Don't go, Frigimon!" Tai called. "You can't catch his cold! You already are!"

Again, Gabumon made a loud honking sneeze.

"How did you get sick?" Tai asked Gabumon. "You're the one with fur around here."

Matt grabbed Tai's arm—hard. "Stop making fun of him!" Matt ordered angrily. "Leave him alone, Tai!"

"Hey!" Tai shouted, yanking his arm free. "Chill out,

Matt! I was trying to see how we could help him!"

When Gabumon sneezed again, Agumon led him back to the cave. "Gabumon," Agumon said worriedly, "I think you ought to rest for a while."

"I *thig* you're right," Gabumon replied, sniffling.

Tai put his hands on his hips. "We have to figure out what we're going to do next," he told Matt.

"Well, isn't it obvious?" Matt snapped. "We have to search for all the others!"

"Yeah, right," Tai replied calmly, "but how are we supposed to do that? Frigimon said that everyone landed on different islands. Unless you've got an airplane stashed around here someplace, we're stuck!"

"So we'll ask Frigimon for help," Matt said.

"Did you not hear me?" Tai asked, getting annoyed. "They're scattered all over the place. Frigimon only has two arms . . . he's not an octopus!"

Matt glared at Tai angrily. "Then I'll have to make a raft out of some of these trees, *okay*?"

Tai grabbed Matt's shoulders. "Calm down!" he said. "Wow, what's eating you? I'll help you get us off this island if we have to build *surfboards*, okay?"

When Matt drooped his head, Tai let go. "Look," Tai said. "The others will be fine without us for now, because we've got to focus on the real deal."

Matt grabbed the front of Tai's blue shirt. "You doofus!" Matt screamed. "There's nothing more real than our friends!" He gave Tai a hard shove. "And finding them!"

The two boys stood face-to-face, with their fists raised.

Gabumon and Agumon rushed out of the cave when they heard the fight. Tai growled as Agumon and Gabumon grabbed him before he could hit Matt.

"You want to ditch your friends to go look for some far-away land?" Matt screamed. "Go ahead, but I'm not coming! I'll find all of them! *By myself!*"

With an angry sob, Matt whirled around and ran into the woods.

"Hey!" Tai shouted, pulling free. He chased Matt across a snow-covered field, gaining on him. "Matt, come on! Don't freak out!"

Matt kept running, but Tai was faster. "You're not getting away that easy!" Tai yelled. Tai lunged and grabbed Matt around the ankles. Both boys landed face-first in the snow.

Tai jumped on top of Matt, holding him down.

"Now, *listen*," Tai said. "Maybe there's something across the ocean to help us find the others! Why do you have to get so bent out of shape? I know how you feel—"

Matt twisted to punch Tai in the face.

Tai toppled off. Agumon gasped and hurried over to Tai's side, quickly followed by Gabumon.

"You haven't got a clue how I feel, Tai!" Matt screamed. "You're acting like such a jerk!"

"Who are you calling a jerk?" Tai demanded. He slammed Matt with another tackle.

"Tai, stop that!" Agumon cried.

Gabumon hopped in alarm. "You have to work together, guys!" he yelled.

But Tai and Matt didn't listen. They rolled in the snow, wrestling furiously.

"What do we do?" Gabumon asked Agumon. "We have to stop them!"

Tai and Matt rolled down the snowy slope, still wrestling. Neither one stayed on top more than a second

before the other pushed him over. They tumbled to a stop near the edge of the cliff. Tai had the upper hand, and he pulled back his arm for a punch— But he stopped when he saw Matt's face.

Tears streamed out of Matt's eyes. "It's T.K.," he sobbed.

Tai lowered his fist.

"He's out there on some strange island," Matt whimpered, "and he's all alone!"

Tai nodded. "That's it," he said softly. "Wow."

Agumon and Gabumon hurried down the hill. "Matt, Tai!" Agumon screamed. "Get away from that cliff!"

"Huh?" Tai grunted. He hadn't noticed how close they were to the edge.

Then, with a rumble, the edge suddenly crumbled away!

"Whoa!" Matt cried.

Tai screamed as he tumbled down, but he didn't panic. With one hand, he grabbed a tree branch sticking out of the cliff. Then he clutched Matt's arm with his other hand.

Up above, Agumon and Gabumon screamed the boys' names.

As Matt's weight hit him, Tai grunted. "I got you!" he

hollered. "Hang on, Matt! Whatever you do, don't let go of my hand!"

"Don't give up, guys!" Agumon called. "Hold on!"

Agumon scrambled partway down the side of the cliff, but it was too sheer. Neither he nor Gabumon could find a firm foothold on the cracked wall.

"It's hopeless," Agumon whined. "I'm so tired and hungry. I don't have any strength left at all!"

"We'd be okay if I could just digivolve into Garurumon!" Gabumon said. He sneezed again. He was too sick.

Just then, choosing the worst moment to attack, a massive monster slid down the slope. The white, hairy creature roared as it rushed closer, wielding an ice spike above his head.

Agumon screamed. "It's Mojyamon!" he shrieked.

"He has a Black Gear in him!" Gabumon shouted. Mojyamon had wooly white fur, and he stood about seven feet tall. He snarled as he hurried toward the Digimon. "Ice Cloud!" Mojyamon roared as he slammed his spike in the ground.

The spike glowed with blue light. Cracks formed at Mojyamon's feet, spreading toward the edge. Then another chunk of the cliff broke off—taking Agumon and Gabumon with it!

The Digimon screamed. They smacked into the branch Tai was holding, cracking it.

All four friends plummeted toward the hard ground far below.

5

As Mojyamon roared triumphantly overhead, Tai, Matt, Agumon, and Gabumon hurtled toward the ground.

Amazingly, Frigimon was strolling underneath them. Tai and Matt fell onto the snowman's head, knocking Frigimon on his back. The snowman dropped everything he'd been carrying. Gabumon and Agumon landed on Frigimon's stomach, bouncing to safety.

"Oof!" Frigimon said. "It's raining kids again. I need to carry an umbrella!"

"Thanks, Frigimon!" Agumon said, climbing out of a snow bank.

Frigimon picked up the objects he'd dropped. "Well, next time try not to land on my head," the snowman said pleasantly. He held out a giant paw full of fruits and vegetables. "Here, I brought some food."

Tai grabbed a bunch of berries. "Excellent, big dude!" he cheered.

"And it's good and tasty—just the way I like it!" Agumon said as he gobbled down a carrot.

Frigimon offered Gabumon a bunch of long grass. "An old cold remedy," the snowman explained.

Gabumon shoved the grass into his mouth and chewed. He gagged and his eyes bugged out from the horrible taste.

Right then, Mojyamon landed behind the group with a roar. The forest creature still had a Black Gear stuck in his chest.

The kids and the Digimons squealed, scrambling into the woods to hide.

"I'll take care of Mojyamon!" Frigimon bellowed.

Mojyamon charged with an echoing howl.

Frigimon smacked Mojyamon with a powerful punch. Mojyamon sailed backward through the air until he crashed into the cliff. The impact left a hole—revealing a bunch of Black Gears!

Mojyamon climbed to his feet and rushed at Frigimon with a snarl.

"Subzero Ice Punch!" Frigimon hollered. He swung at Mojyamon, but the monster ducked and grabbed

Frigimon's arm. Then Mojyamon flipped Frigimon over his shoulder.

In the woods, the kids and the Digimon gasped as their friend was flattened.

Mojyamon heard the gasps, and glanced around until he saw their hiding spot. "Boomerang Bone!" Mojyamon screamed. He whizzed a grayish bone at their heads.

Agumon and Gabumon threw themselves down onto the snow, and Tai and Matt ducked just in time. The bone whirled around and returned to Mojyamon's claw.

Tai jumped out of the woods. "Nice trick, Mojyamon!" he hollered. "Now watch *ours*!"

The Digivice strapped to his wrist glowed.

Agumon stepped up beside Tai. "Agumon, digivolve to . . . Greymon!" he shouted.

The whole world warped. Brilliant streams of data buzzed through the air, and Agumon exploded with electric energy. He had been a cute little mini-dinosaur, but now he transformed into a Triceratops standing on his hind legs. A leather mask protected his eyes and head.

Gabumon strode toward Mojyamon. "Gabumon, digivolve into . . . Garurumon!"

In another blast of lightning, the fuzzy little Digimon changed into a mixture of an awesome white tiger and an eagle.

Garurumon leaped at Mojyamon, opening his enormous feathered wings.

Mojyamon hurled his Boomerang Bone, but Garurumon caught it in his teeth—and crunched it to splinters.

Heave-ho!

Frigimon proves he's not so coldhearted after all.

Tai and Matt spark up the old rivalry . . .

. . . but nothing can come between true friends for very long

Sukamon and Chuumon yuk it up!!

Centarumon faces off against
Togemon and Kabuterimon.

Izzy finds himself in a thorny situation.

Even Leomon is no match
for Digivice power!

Ogremon's teeth and nails are truly a fright!

Trick or treat?

Bakemon's henchmen reveal what they're really made of.

Meanwhile, Greymon took a deep breath and roared out a huge ball of flame. The glowing fireball soared at Mojyamon.

But at the last second Mojyamon jumped out of the way. Then he kicked Greymon, knocking him onto his side with a heavy thud.

"You're not playing nice," Greymon growled.

Mojyamon snarled at Greymon, but then he squealed as someone grabbed him from behind.

It was Frigimon! "Now!" the snowman instructed. "Aim for the Black Gear in his chest!"

"Nova Blast!" Greymon shouted. This time, Greymon's fireball smacked Mojyamon dead-on. Both he and Frigimon slammed against the cliff.

The wall shattered, raining rocks down on the monsters.

The Black Gear popped out of Mojyamon's chest and disintegrated in a wisp of poisonous smoke.

Mojyamon shrunk down to his normal size—not much bigger than the kids.

"That's more like it!" Frigimon said. Then he noticed Garurumon peering at something. "Garurumon," the snowman asked, "what are you looking at?"

Garurumon let out a gust of his Howling Blaster attack. The blue flame scorched all the Black Gears in the hole, crumbling them.

"Wow, look at all those Gears," Matt said. "There's a mountain of them!"

After Garurumon shrank back into Gabumon, and Greymon changed back into Agumon, Mojyamon woke up. "Whoa, what happened?" he asked groggily. "I feel like I was run over by a Monochromon!"

"You had a Black Gear controlling you, Mojyamon," Agumon explained.

"The same thing happened to me," Frigimon said. He picked up the shrunken Mojyamon and placed him on his frozen shoulder. "It's okay, no one got hurt."

Matt poked Tai in the arm. "This doesn't change anything," he said. "We still have to find the others—"

With a gasp, Matt pointed at the cliff. Blue lightning was shooting out of the Black Gears as they began to regenerate. As the repaired Gears started turning, the whole island shuddered with a powerful lurch.

"The island's moving again," Matt noticed.

Tai pulled out his spyglass and peered across the ocean. "We're moving, all right," he agreed. "The other way! Back toward Infinity Mountain!"

"And Devimon," Matt added worriedly.

"If that's true," Tai said, "this is no time for us to be fighting."

Matt nodded. He and Tai grasped hands, calling a truce.

Tai laughed happily. "No stinking Gears are going to stop us!" he yelled.

"Yeah!" Matt cheered. "Together we're going to be all right!"

Part

11

ADVENTURE IN GREAT CANYON

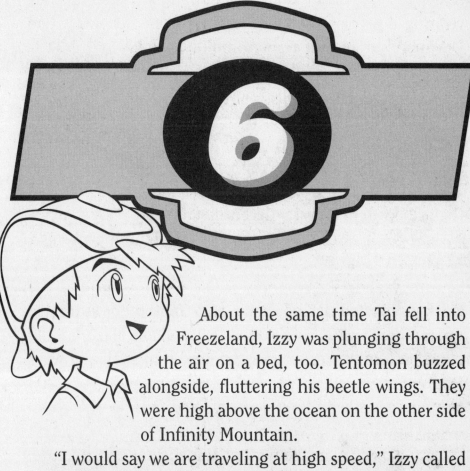

6

About the same time Tai fell into Freezeland, Izzy was plunging through the air on a bed, too. Tentomon buzzed alongside, fluttering his beetle wings. They were high above the ocean on the other side of Infinity Mountain.

"I would say we are traveling at high speed," Izzy called to Tentomon, "plummeting toward an unidentified island!

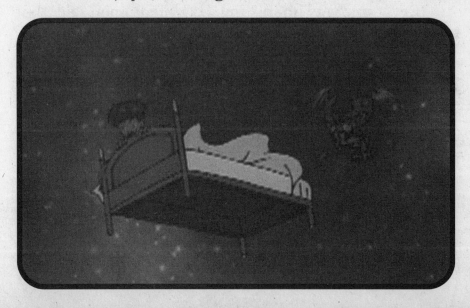

And . . . uh . . . crash-landing is imminent!" Izzy was only wearing a pair of shorts, since he'd been sleeping when Devimon hurled him away from File Island.

"Try to think of it as hitting the beach!" Tentomon called to Izzy. He swooped down as the bed fell toward a dense forest on the island. With Tentomon pulling on the headboard and Izzy leaning his weight to one side, they steered the bed over the tops of the jungle trees. When Tentomon spotted a small clearing up ahead, they guided the bed down to a pretty decent landing.

Izzy got dressed quickly, and he and Tentomon set out to explore the area.

After wandering for only a few minutes around the thickly forested island, Izzy and Tentomon stumbled upon an ancient city in ruins. In the main plaza, an old stone building sat covered with vines. It had tall archways leading in to it, filled with dark shadows. Izzy and Tentomon walked along a rocky road over to the abandoned building.

Izzy gaped in amazement at the ancient architecture. "Whoa," he murmured, awed.

"Er . . . yes, very interesting, Izzy," Tentomon said, "but don't you think we should keep searching for the others? I mean, now really isn't the time to—"

"I know," Izzy interrupted. "But just look at this place . . . it's *prodigious*! I've got to check it out, Tentomon, just for a minute." Then Izzy ducked through one of the ruin's archways, disappearing inside.

Tentomon buzzed after Izzy. "All right," he sighed, "but just for a minute."

Meanwhile, Mimi and Palmon were crashing on another island not far away. They both screamed as their bed smacked down in the middle of a hot jungle. Mimi was only wearing a nightgown. She climbed off the bed, pushing the jungle's vines away from her. "Now that trip should be good for some frequent-flyer miles!" she grumbled, getting dressed in her pink cowgirl outfit. As she put on her hat, Mimi cried out in dismay. "Oh, no!" she wailed. "Humidity!"

"Yes," Palmon said. She looked basically like a white

radish with legs, but she could be fierce. "This is a tropical rain forest, but not one I'm familiar with. It all happened so fast, I don't know where we are."

Mimi let out a dramatic sob. "Do you have any idea what humidity does to my hair?" she whined. "It, like, goes all *poodley*! Not a pretty sight!"

"Uh," Palmon said, "perhaps we ought to look around for any of the others."

"Let's go," Mimi agreed. She started walking down a path through the tropical trees. "Maybe we can find some air conditioning."

Mimi and Palmon hiked deep into the overgrown,

damp jungle. Mimi was starting to get grouchy from hunger when she spotted a bunch of purple fruit hanging from a tree branch.

"Yum, bananas!" Mimi exclaimed.

"Huh?" Palmon asked, confused. "Ba-na-nas?" She had never seen them before—yellow *or* purple.

Mimi pointed up at the fruit. "Grab them down, will you?" she begged. "Can you reach high enough?"

"Sure!" Palmon replied. Her vine arms stretched to grab the bananas, and she yanked them down.

"Yay!" Mimi cheered. "Oh man, I was starving!" She peeled the fruit. "Now we can pretend we're having banana splits, huh, Palmon?"

But when Mimi pulled down the last peel, she found nothing inside—it was empty! "What's the big idea?" she complained.

"They certainly do look delicious!" Palmon exclaimed. She grabbed the peels and jammed them into her mouth with a chomp.

Mimi threw her arms wide. "I can't believe it!" she howled, furious. "This place is seriously getting on my nerves!"

Just as Mimi had stopped yelling and had trailed off into sad whimpers, something plopped down next to her. It had fallen from a nearby tree.

Mimi peered down at the pile of pink glop. "Hair mousse?" she wondered. Then she caught a whiff. "Yuck!" she hollered, grossed out.

"Huh?" Palmon said. She inspected the steaming pink pile. "Ew!"

A dopey chuckle came from the tree.

Mimi glanced up. A yellow creature with lots of teeth around his whole body was clinging to a limb. He was fat and mushy, and a tiny mouse sat on his head, holding on to a soft knob.

"Duh . . ." the yellow creature said in a stupid voice. "Good-bye! Meet to nice you!"

"He means *hello*," the little mouse translated. "Nice to meet you!"

A freaked-out expression flickered in Mimi's eyes. "Palmon," she whispered, "who's the talking dessert?"

"It's Sukamon and Chuumon," Palmon replied, "also known as the Digilosers."

"Hey, thanks!" Sukamon and Chuumon called down cheerfully.

"Sukamon and his mouse buddy are always together," Palmon explained to Mimi, "because they share the same teeny-tiny brain."

"That's right!" Sukamon bellowed, suddenly looking very proud of himself. He pelted more of the pink sludge down at Mimi and Palmon.

Mimi screamed. "Run!" she shouted as she took off.

Sukamon followed, jumping from branch to branch. With every jump, he threw a fresh pile of slime. Chuumon rode on Sukamon's head, chittering loudly at Mimi and Palmon.

After another chunk of sludge barely missed her, Mimi wheeled around. "All right!" she shrieked. "That's enough, leave us alone!" Holding a lump of slime, Sukamon halted on a limb. "Heh!" he grunted. "Sure, okay . . . but first you got to pay a whattayacallit!"

"Pay a toll!" Chuumon squeaked.

"Yeah," Sukamon screeched, pointing at Mimi. "Does she think she can just use our woods for free? She's got to pay! Like that, uh . . . *purse* there."

"I like the hat," Chuumon added.

Mimi clutched her purse and pressed her hat down. "No!" she yelled.

"Huh?" Sukamon and Chuumon grunted, confused.

"What part of *no* don't you understand, you whacka-zoids?" Mimi screamed. "Get out of here!"

"I think she insulted us," Chuumon whispered to his mushy friend.

"She did?" Sukamon muttered. He whipped down more hunks of sludge.

"Yeah!" Chuumon cheered. "Go ahead, let her have it!"

Mimi screamed and zoomed away.

Sukamon and Chuumon laughed as they hurried after her, hopping through the treetops.

After running for dozens of yards, Mimi grabbed onto a tree and leaned against it, exhausted. "Oh, that's it, I give up," she moaned, closing her eyes. "I want to see the camp therapist."

Sukamon slid down the tree Mimi was leaning

against. He chuckled softly as he reached for the Digivice attached to the strap of Mimi's purse. "Ooh, pretty," Sukamon said.

When Sukamon touched Mimi's Digivice, it glowed brightly. An explosion of white and yellow light surrounded Sukamon and Chuumon. Zapped, Sukamon stumbled backward, his eyes rolling.

Mimi looked up in surprise as Sukamon reeled around. Chuumon had a dazed look on his mousy face, too.

"Wow, that was better than chewing tin foil!" Sukamon exclaimed, smiling broadly. "I feel all tingly and refreshed, like a whole new person!"

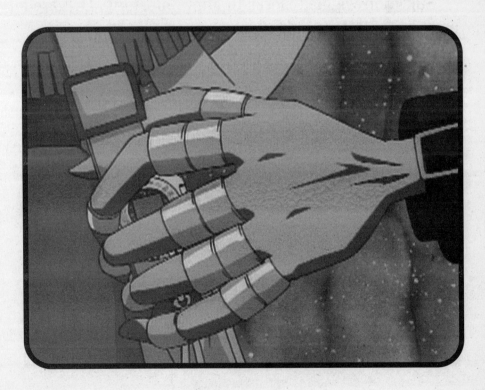

"Yeah," Chuumon chimed in. "We're a whole new person!"

Mimi stared at the Digilosers. "Is this person as much of a pain as the last one?" she asked.

"No, really," Sukamon said happily, "we'll be nice from now on!"

"So you'll leave us alone?" Mimi demanded.

"Wait!" Palmon said. "First tell us if you've seen any other humans."

"Any what?" Sukamon asked dopily.

Palmon pointed at Mimi. "Creatures that look like this one," she explained.

Sukamon wiggled closer to Mimi, blushing. He gazed up at her with love in his eyes.

"Duh, well, it wasn't nearly as pretty as you are, of course," he replied, "but we saw *something* fall into the old ruins with a Tentomon."

"So, when were you planning on telling us, next week?" Mimi snapped. Then she smiled at Palmon. "They must've seen Izzy, too!"

"Listen, you two, can you take us there?" Palmon asked. "It's important that we find him."

Sukamon grinned. "Okey-dokey!" he said.

Mimi and Palmon followed the Digilosers as they hopped through the jungle. In a short while, they reached

a clearing at the island's edge. The other island was close by—its cliff was across a thin strip of sea.

"Right over there!" Sukamon called, pointing to the other island.

"Oh, that's just great!" Mimi cried, as she stared at the forest on the other side. "How are we supposed to get over there?"

"You're the one with the big hat," Chuumon squeaked.

"You think of something. A gorgeous girl like you must have a big brain!"

"Thanks a lot," Mimi replied flatly. "Really."

Sukamon let out a goofy chuckle. "Before you go," he

asked shyly, "maybe you could give us a thank-you kiss, huh?" He puckered up his gross lips.

"Oh, please tell me they're kidding," Mimi hissed to Palmon.

Palmon stepped to the edge. Then she stretched her vine arms all the way to the next island. Palmon grabbed a tree on the other side. "Climb aboard!"

Mimi threw her arms around Palmon.

They swung over the water and landed safely on the other island's cliff. Palmon shrunk her arms to normal size again.

"Blah!" Mimi cried. "Just the *thought* of that kiss is making me queasy."

Sukamon cupped his hands around his mouth. "That's okay," he called. "We'll wait till you come back!"

"Don't hold your breath!" Mimi replied.

Then she and Palmon blew the Digilosers a loud, rude raspberry.

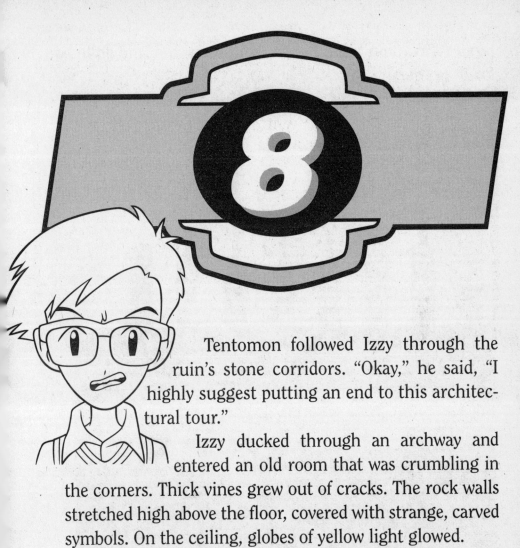

Tentomon followed Izzy through the ruin's stone corridors. "Okay," he said, "I highly suggest putting an end to this architectural tour."

Izzy ducked through an archway and entered an old room that was crumbling in the corners. Thick vines grew out of cracks. The rock walls stretched high above the floor, covered with strange, carved symbols. On the ceiling, globes of yellow light glowed.

"I am gathering information," Izzy replied. "I'm sure this place is crawling with clues." He pointed at a cog sticking out of the floor. "Look," Izzy said excitedly, "it's one of Devimon's Black Gears!"

"So it is," Tentomon said. The Black Gear was taller than both of them, and it turned slowly.

"Know what I think?" Izzy asked. "I think if we stop this Gear turning, we'll completely jam up that creep Devimon."

"Or, even better, we could *not* do that," Tentomon replied. "Wouldn't that be fun? And then we could go look for the others."

Izzy examined the symbols. "Wait a minute," he muttered, "this is the same writing we saw the last time. Remember?"

Tentomon nodded—he totally recalled the mysterious writing they'd found inside a giant battery.

Izzy sat down in front of the rock wall and opened his laptop. "It made me realize that in DigiWorld, basic data is a living, viable substance," he continued. "All the data's stored on my hard drive." Izzy glanced around. "If only there was a power source nearby . . ."

"Get a power source, stop the Gear . . ." Tentomon complained. "Is *find our friends* on that list?"

"Those lights are getting power from somewhere," Izzy murmured, not really listening to Tentomon. He spotted a

pronged opening attached to a nearby root. "Hey, an out-let!"

Izzy plugged in his laptop. "Check it out," he said. Three pineapples flashed on his screen. "It works!"

"Wonderful," Tentomon muttered.

Izzy hunched over the laptop, facing the writing on the wall. "Now let's see if I can decipher this," he said.

Mimi and Palmon quickly located the ancient plaza hidden in the jungle. "Here are the old ruins," Mimi announced. "Let's hope that kissy-face lemon custard was telling the truth."

"One way to find out," Palmon said. She strode through the nearest archway, and Mimi hurried after her.

It wasn't long before they found the room where Izzy had set up his laptop. "Over there!" Mimi exclaimed. "It's them! Hi!"

Izzy barely glanced up. "Hey, Mimi," he said.

"Finally, a friendly face!" Mimi chirped. "Where's the rest of the gang?"

"I have no idea," Izzy answered. This time he didn't look up at all.

"But, uh . . . shouldn't we search for them?" Mimi asked. She peered over his shoulder at the screen, which was filled with bizarre symbols. "What're you doing anyway?"

"Right now," Izzy said, "I'm trying to decipher these hieroglyphs."

"Can't that wait?" Mimi asked.

"That's what I keep telling him," Tentomon said. "But does he listen to me? No."

Mimi squeezed her hands into fists. "All right," she insisted. "Get up, Izzy!"

Izzy kept typing. "I'm sure the key to figuring out everything is in here, if I can only find it," he muttered. "But does each glyph represent a letter, a word, or a phrase? I'll have to cross-reference the characteristics . . ."

Relaxing her fists, Mimi let out an exasperated sigh. Then she plopped down beside Palmon to wait for Izzy to finish.

A long while later, they were still waiting. "Izzy, any

idea how long this is going to take?" Mimi asked. "I mean, can we go sometime before winter sets in?"

"Oh, wait," Izzy murmured, staring at his screen. "Yeah, that might work." He started typing again.

With a furious grunt, Mimi jumped to her feet. "Are you ignoring me, you computer geek pipsqueak?" she hollered.

"Okay," Izzy muttered, "so if I make the variable constant and search for vowel patterns . . ."

Mimi started shaking like she was about to explode. Her lips trembled, and her eyes grew very wide. There was nothing she hated more than being ignored!

"Hey! Here's something!" Izzy exclaimed. A map

popped up on his screen. "Whoa, prodigious!" he said. "These ruins are a giant maze!"

"All right, I'm leaving!" Mimi shrieked. She burst into sobs. "Right now!" Hot tears streamed down her face.

Izzy turned around to blink at Mimi in surprise.

Palmon started crying, too, sniffling.

"Don't cry, Mimi!" Tentomon said. "Izzy, tell her you're sorry!"

"Sorry?" Izzy asked. "For what?"

"I can't take it anymore!" Mimi wailed. "I haven't had

anything to eat and my feet are killing me and a giant lemon custard tried to kiss me and all I want to do is to get out of here!" She let out a fresh burst of sobs.

"We want to leave!" Palmon bawled. "Is that so wrong?" She hurried over to Izzy. "Honestly," Palmon scolded him, "how can you be so insensitive?" She pointed at the laptop. "You just ignore us while you poke away at your computer!"

"I'm not ignoring you!" Izzy protested. "I'm doing something ultra-important, like maybe saving this world. If I can just decipher these hieroglyphs, then maybe we could—"

"Oh, you can keep your stupid hieroglyphs!" Mimi interrupted. She blubbered as she rushed out of the room.

"Mimi! Wait!" Tentomon called. He buzzed after her into the corridor.

Palmon faced Izzy angrily. "Admit it," she said, "you just like playing on your computer, that's all!"

"You think I'm just playing around here?" Izzy asked, insulted.

"I almost think you like computers more than people!" Palmon yelled. Then she started to cry again.

Izzy glanced behind him, and his eyes widened. "Don't look now, but Mimi and Tentomon are gone."

Palmon's tears dried up instantly. "Now what do we do?" she asked grimly.

"They didn't go deeper into the maze, did they?" Izzy asked.

"That'd be my guess," Palmon replied.

Izzy shook his head, worried. "These deciphered hieroglyphs tell me the inside of these ruins is a giant labyrinth," he explained. "So in that case . . ." Izzy gulped. "They could be lost in there forever."

"Forever?" Palmon gasped.

9

Palmon paced next to Izzy's laptop. "Ooh, I can't stand it!" she squealed. "I'm going in after them!"

"And get lost, too?" Izzy replied as he typed away on his keyboard. "No, Palmon. We've got to use our heads first."

"But we can't just leave them!" Palmon protested.

"We won't," Izzy promised, "but this is one super-complicated maze. I've got to try to get a handle on it, then maybe I can help get them out."

Suddenly a red square flickered on his map, blinking as it moved slowly along a twisty route on the screen. "There they are," Izzy said. He slid his cursor over to the square and clicked on it.

The laptop's radio squawked. "No, no, not that way," said Tentomon's tinny-sounding voice.

"Oh, buzz off," Mimi snapped. "Leave me alone!"

Palmon smiled. "That's my girl!" she exclaimed.

"I've homed in on the signal from her Digivice," Izzy explained as he put on a headset microphone. "We can hear her. Now let's hope she can hear us."

"Hey, Mimi, do you read me?" he asked. "Testing, testing!"

"Izzy?" Mimi replied. "Is that you? Help us, we're lost in this stupid maze! And your Digimon keeps telling me it's *my* fault!"

"What do you know, it works!" Izzy cheered. "Okay, Mimi, I'm going to navigate for you. Take the first doorway on the right," he instructed. "When you get to the end, turn left. But be careful of the next room, because there's a hole in the floor."

Mimi followed his directions, and entered an empty chamber with sturdy stone walls. The floor was made of stone, too, but when Mimi stepped inside, it suddenly crumbled in front of her, revealing a deep pit. She jumped back, startled.

"There should be a narrow ledge you can use to get across," Izzy told her.

Carefully, Mimi began to inch along the ledge around the pit. "Izzy, did we have to take the scenic route?" she asked.

On Izzy's screen, a glowing blue dot appeared a few rooms behind Mimi's red square. "Uh-oh," he said.

"What do you mean, *uh-oh*?" Palmon demanded.

"I was hoping it was just a glitch," Izzy replied. "But there's definitely something in that maze with them, and it's getting closer."

Palmon pressed her leafy hands to her chest. "Now I am starting to worry."

76

Mimi passed the pit and entered another long hallway. "I'm ready," she told Izzy. "Which way should we go? What's with the silent treatment?"

Then she flinched as she heard a nasty chuckle behind her.

"Did you hear that?" Tentomon asked nervously. "It sounded evil."

Turning around slowly, Mimi saw an orange creature walking toward her. He had a man's head and chest, with the legs and body of a horse, and he was covered in purple armor. Mimi gasped as she spotted the Black Gear sticking out of his back.

"Oh, no!" Tentomon cried. "Centarumon! He's half-man, half-horse . . . and you really don't want to get on either one of his bad sides! Run!"

Mimi ran. Tentomon swooped behind her down the long hallway.

"I like a good chase!" Centarumon bellowed. He galloped after them.

"Left!" Izzy called over the radio. "Take a left!"

Mimi and Tentomon hurried to follow his instructions. They rushed down another hall, but slowed as they came to a fork in the corridor.

"Another left!" Izzy told them. "Through the doorway!"

"This way, Mimi!" Tentomon cried as he zoomed under an arch. He led her into another empty room with stone walls . . . but there was no way out!

"Great job, Izzy!" Mimi exclaimed. "It's a dead end!"

"Where do we go now?" Tentomon asked. He waited a moment and got no reply. "Izzy? Hello? We seem to have lost contact with him!"

"Oh, really?" Centarumon said.

Tentomon waved his insect arms in terror. "He's back!"

"Solar Ray!" Centarumon shouted. He held out his arm, and a panel in his palm slid open. A flash of bright flame shot at Mimi's head.

Tentomon knocked Mimi out of the way. The blast hit the wall behind her, cracking the stone.

"What are you waiting for?" Mimi asked Tentomon. "Make yourself bigger!"

"Oh, I'd love to digivolve!" Tentomon replied. "But if I'm separated from Izzy, that's impossible—"

The entire room suddenly shook like somebody had driven a bulldozer into the side of the building. Dust billowed out from the trembling stone walls.

"What's that racket?" Tentomon wondered.

Behind him, more cracks appeared in the wall. Stones tumbled into the room. Bright sunlight poured in, and Izzy and Palmon stepped inside.

"Get out of there!" Izzy shouted. "Hurry, come on!"

"You don't have to tell me twice!" Mimi chirped.

But Centarumon strode closer, blocking the exit with his giant horse's body.

"Watch out, Mimi!" Palmon cried. "Palmon, digivolve into . . . Togemon!"

A digital explosion rocked the ruins. Sizzling bolts of energy swirled around Palmon as she transformed from a little walking radish into a giant barrel cactus. Her claws changed into huge boxing gloves.

Then Tentomon stepped forward. "Leave this to me!" he yelled. "Tentomon digivolve into . . . Kabuterimon!"

The cute beetle-like Digimon glowed with energy and transformed into a scary-looking dragonfly.

That's when Centarumon shot another Solar Blast attack. It hit the transformed Digimon, who shielded

Mimi and Izzy. All four of them were knocked right through the wall! They tumbled into the plaza, crashing on the ground outside.

"That's one way to get out of there," Mimi said. She waved smoke out of her face.

"Yeah," Izzy agreed, "but this is no time to start taking it easy. Look who's here!"

Centarumon galloped out of the hole, stampeding toward Mimi and Izzy.

"Leave them alone!" Kabuterimon shouted, jumping between Centarumon and the kids. "Electro Shocker!" He hurled a light blue and purple ball of energy.

Togemon stood up, too. "I think it's time for . . . Needle Spray!" she hollered. Her sharp spines sprang off her cactus body.

Their two attacks combined in the air, doubling in strength before they walloped Centarumon. He staggered from the mighty blow. The Black Gear popped out of his back, and disintegrated into greasy fumes.

"That felt . . . interesting," Centarumon muttered. He slumped over.

Togemon shrunk back to Palmon, and Kabuterimon transformed into Tentomon again.

Centarumon was unconscious for only a second. "Where am I?" he asked groggily.

Mimi walked over to him. "Are you a good Digimon now?" she asked.

Centarumon glanced at her purse, and his eyes grew wide. "What? That device, on your bag!"

"This?" Mimi asked, showing him the Digivice attached to her purse strap.

"I have seen it before," Centarumon said. While the little Digimons waited outside, he quickly led the kids into the ruins and brought them to a secret room. On the wall over a stone altar there was a gigantic carving shaped like a Digivice.

"It is a mystical symbol," Centarumon explained. "These ruins are its temple, and I am its guardian. The Digivice is a preserver of the light—a last line of defense against the darkness that threatens existence."

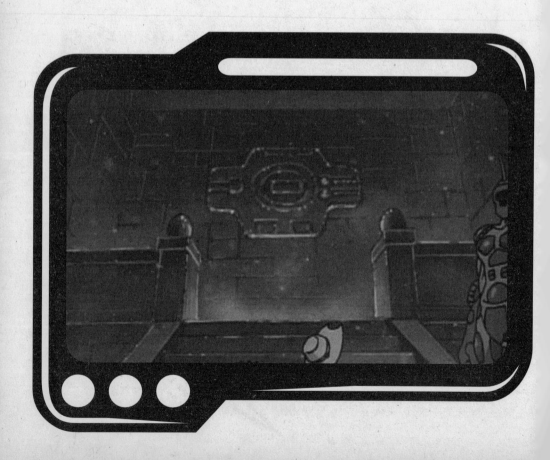

"I didn't get a word of that," Mimi said, "but I'm beginning to think they're more than just a cool accessory."

The sound of footsteps echoed behind her, and Centarumon's eyes grew wide. "Leomon?" he asked. "Why are you here?"

Mimi and Izzy whirled around. On the top of Infinity Mountain, Leomon had protected the kids from Devimon. But then Devimon had caught Leomon in a spell, enslaving him and making him evil.

Leomon pounced into the room. His eyes had the gaze of a zombie.

"To destroy the children," Leomon replied.

10

Mimi and Izzy gasped in terror. Leomon had a lion's head on a totally buff human body. He glared at Centarumon, growling. "I warn you, do not interfere with me," he threatened. Then he leaped over to Mimi and Izzy in a single bound.

"No!" Centarumon cried. He galloped over to Leomon to block him from getting to the kids. Leomon swung at Centarumon with a vicious punch.

Mimi screamed. "I can't look, it's just too scary!" she shrieked, covering her eyes with her hands. But then she spread her fingers. "Well, maybe a peep."

Centarumon caught Leomon's punch in his own hand. "I said no, Leomon!" he shouted. "The children possess the Digivice. As the guardian of its temple, I must protect them as well."

Leomon pushed Centarumon aside. "Ha!" he laughed. "Protect them from me? Good luck!" He swung at Centarumon again, shouting, "Fist of the Beast King!"

Centarumon jumped over Leomon, out of harm's way. "Solar Ray!" he hollered. A tongue of fire flashed out of Centarumon's palm, blasting Leomon to the ground.

Leomon leaped up quickly, barely injured.

"Now," Centarumon said, "let's stop this madness before one of us is hurt."

In reply to the offer, Leomon let out a big roar . . . and pounced at Centarumon. He slammed him against a stone

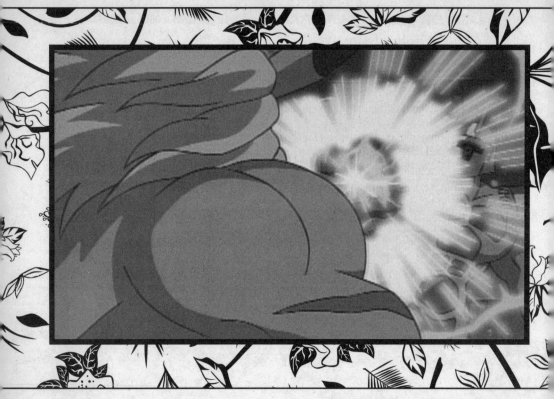

wall with a wild punch. Centarumon hit the stone so hard that he left a dent in his shape. He slumped to the floor, knocked out.

Mimi and Izzy both screamed—their protector had been flattened!

Leomon turned to the kids, his eyes swirling with emptiness. "The children must be destroyed," he said flatly.

"You must mean some other children!" Mimi squealed. She raised her purse in front of her face, hiding behind it.

Leomon groaned in pain as the Digivice attached to Mimi's purse glowed.

"Hey, your Digivice!" Izzy called. "It stopped him in his tracks!" He held up his own Digivice, pointing it at the brainwashed Digimon. Brilliant rays sprang out at Leomon, who backed away.

"Bad kitty!" Mimi screeched, holding up her gleaming Digivice. "Out! Go on, out!"

With a frightened growl, Leomon turned and ran. He rushed up a flight of stairs, escaping deeper into the maze.

Centarumon climbed painfully to his feet.

"Well, that got rid of Leomon," Mimi chirped. She smiled down at her Digivice. "These things really are kind of amazing."

"A preserver of the light against the darkness," Izzy whispered, repeating Centarumon's words.

"Can you order a pizza with it?" Mimi joked. "I'm still starving!"

Centarumon, Izzy, and Mimi met up with Tentomon

and Palmon in the room with all the writing on the wall. Izzy showed Centarumon the Gear turning slowly in the corner.

"Maybe with your help we could stop this Black Gear," Izzy said.

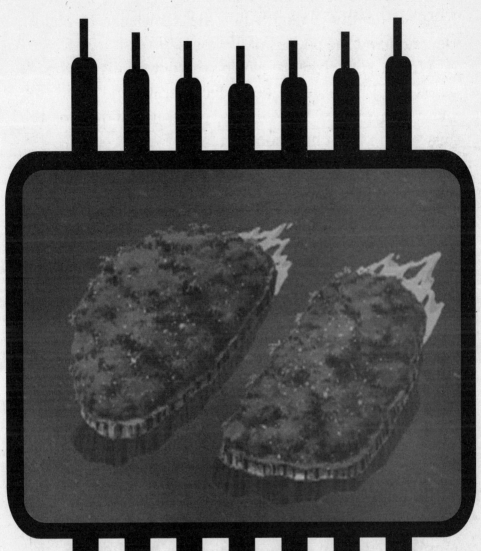

Centarumon shook his head sadly. "No," he replied, "I have neither the strength nor the knowledge to oppose Devimon and the powers of darkness."

With a sigh, Izzy sat down in front of his laptop. "I guess I'll just have to keep deciphering and analyzing these two sets of hieroglyphs," he said. "I'm sure the answers are all in here somewhere."

Mimi stamped her foot. "You're not seriously starting all that again!" she demanded angrily.

"Just a nano," Izzy replied as he began to type.

Mimi strode over to the Black Gear and gave it a sharp kick. "Who cares about this dumb old thing?" she grumbled. "All I want is lunch!"

Palmon gasped in astonishment as the Gear stopped turning for a second. It quickly started up again . . . whirling in the opposite direction!

Everybody rushed out of the ruins, hurrying through the jungle to the island's edge. The broken piece of File Island was now slowly floating back toward Infinity Mountain!

"Look, the process has reversed itself!" Izzy exclaimed.

"Amazing!" Palmon said.

The island sailed gracefully past the first island where Mimi and Palmon had originally landed. Mimi groaned when she spotted a familiar mushy yellow figure hopping on the other side of the water.

"Hiya!" Sukamon called, waving. "I knew you couldn't keep away!"

Digivolve holiday ornaments into supercool Digimon decorations!

Choose dove or flying crane origami, then cut out the origami paper on the next page and start folding!

DOVE Origami

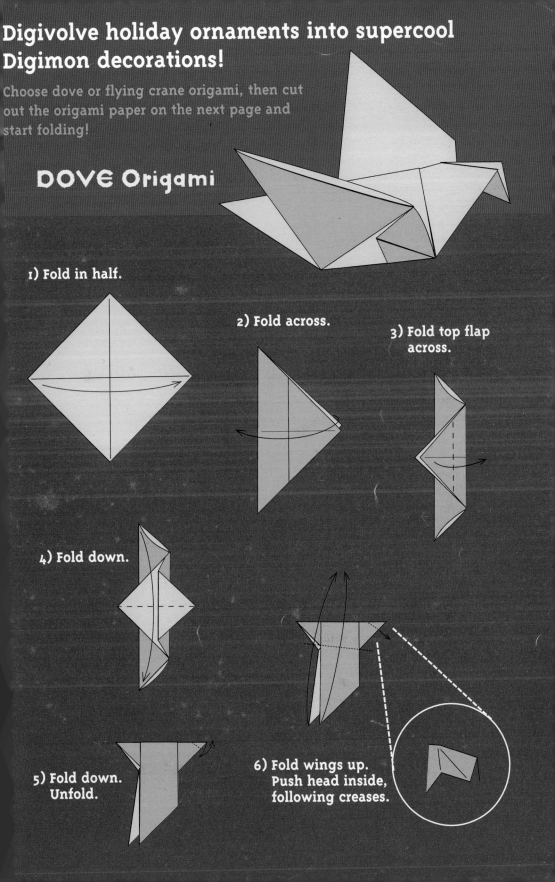

1) Fold in half.

2) Fold across.

3) Fold top flap across.

4) Fold down.

5) Fold down. Unfold.

6) Fold wings up. Push head inside, following creases.

FLYING CRANE Origami

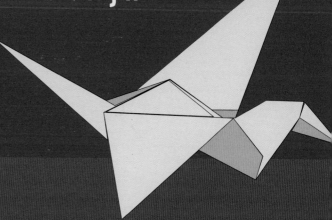

1) Fold in half.

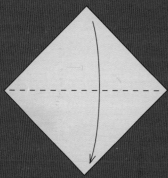

2) Fold in half again.

3) Fold down top flap to make crease and unfold again. Open flap

4) Smooth top edge down.

5) Repeat steps 3 and 4 on backside.

6) Fold top and side corners in. Unfold. Repeat on backside.

7) Open flap and pull up. Press flat along creases. Repeat on backside.

8) Fold up. Unfold.

9) Following creases, push inner edges inside out.

10) Fold down wings. Push edge inside to make beak.

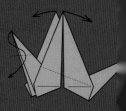

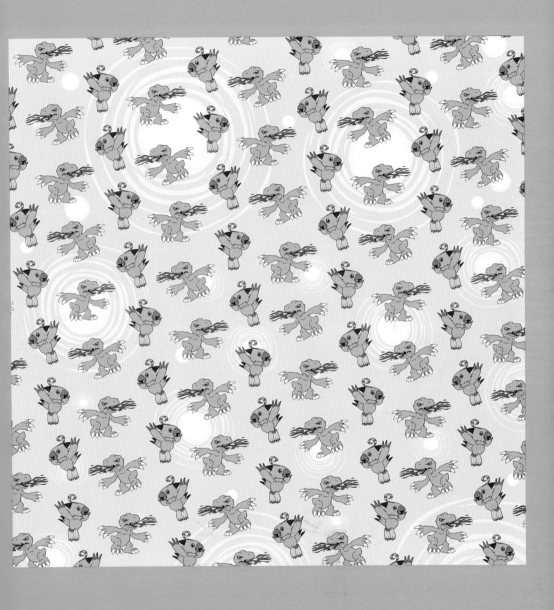

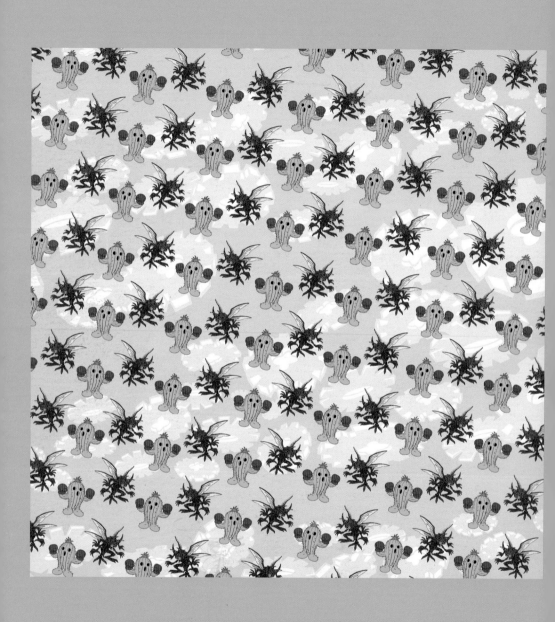

WISHING YOU A HOLIDAY THAT'S OUT OF THIS WORLD!

Chuumon laughed from atop Sukamon's head.

Mimi glanced at Palmon. "Ew!" they both exclaimed, wrinkling their noses.

"At least blow us a kiss!" Sukamon shouted.

Mimi and Palmon shared a smile, and then faced the Digilosers. "All right!" Mimi called.

And she and Palmon blew Sukamon another loud, rude raspberry.

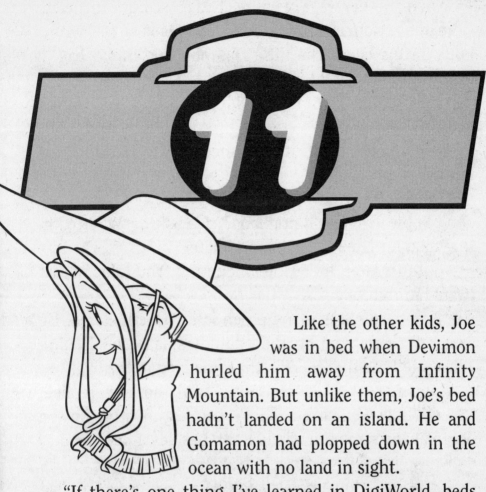

11

Like the other kids, Joe was in bed when Devimon hurled him away from Infinity Mountain. But unlike them, Joe's bed hadn't landed on an island. He and Gomamon had plopped down in the ocean with no land in sight.

"If there's one thing I've learned in DigiWorld, beds don't make good boats," Joe moaned. He slumped over the headboard, feeling seasick. "Yuck."

When another wave of nausea had passed, Joe turned to Gomamon. Gomamon looked like a white baby seal with a horn on his head. The little Digimon dug into a bag of food, munching and humming.

"*What?*" Joe screamed. "Did I just hear you eating *again*?"

Gomamon looked at Joe sheepishly. "Uh-huh," he replied.

"Didn't I tell you not to eat up all the food, since we don't know when we'll find land?" Joe asked. "We need to save food for later . . . as in *much* later!"

"But it is later, Joe," Gomamon said. "You told me that twenty minutes ago."

"Twenty minutes is not much later!" Joe hollered. He grabbed Gomamon by the shoulders and shook him. "Please tell me that there's still some food in the bag!"

Gomamon smiled nervously. "Well, no," he replied. "Seeing how you can't handle eating and floating on the ocean at the same time, I ate it all. Besides, I need food to digivolve, in case we run into bad Digimons."

Joe shook Gomamon again. "Have we seen any bad Digimons?" Joe asked. "No! If I starve, who are you going to protect?"

Then another ripple of seasickness hit Joe. He hugged Gomamon to his chest as he started to feel barfy. With a gagging groan, Joe hurried to the headboard and puked into the water.

"That's enough talk about food," Gomamon said. He

rubbed Joe's back with his clawed flipper. "Things will get better soon. Hang in there, buddy."

Joe glanced up and saw a wooden crate bobbing toward the bed.

"That crate is going to hit us!" Gomamon cried.

Joe gasped, but his fear turned to excitement as he thought about what might be inside the crate. "Maybe it's full of fruit, veggies, bread, milk, cereal, hamburgers, hot dogs, cookies, candy, and soda!" he exclaimed, peering at the crate as it floated closer. "Looks like I'll need a jack-hammer to open this. Let's see . . ."

The crate burst open, splintering.

Joe screamed when he saw that a big, nasty green Digimon was hiding inside!

"Ogremon!" Gomamon shrieked. Ogremon was Devimon's meanest henchman, and he looked like a monster you'd be terrified of finding under the bed.

"None other, you little Digipest!" Ogremon replied. He raised a wooden club above his head. "Pummel Whack!" he yelled, whipping the club at Joe and Gomamon. They ducked under Ogremon's club as he swung it at them.

When he aimed for their feet, Joe and Gomamon jumped over the club, screaming.

When he saw that Joe and Gomamon weren't easy targets, Ogremon aimed for the bed. "Pummel Whack!" he hollered again, bashing the mattress. The bed cracked in two pieces, and Joe and Gomamon were thrown into the air.

As Gomamon fell toward the water, he shouted, "Come out of the sea, Marching Fishes!"

On his command, dozens of multicolored fish flipped out of the ocean, flinging themselves at Ogremon. "I'm not scared of some stinking fish!" Ogremon shouted, waving his club over his head. Then a fish smacked him in the face. "On second thought," he said, "that really hurt!"

With a loud holler, Ogremon punched the fish out of the sky. They splashed back into the sea, and Ogremon stood up in the crate. He raised his club to swing it at Joe.

Joe cringed, waiting for the blow to hit.

"Gomamon digivolve to . . . Ikkakumon!" Gomamon shouted.

The water churned and swirls of digital data flashed as Gomamon transformed into a huge wooly walrus with a sharp horn on his head.

The amazing transformation interrupted Ogremon's attack. The ocean churned around Ikkakumon, supporting his massive body on the waves.

"You're bigger now!" Ogremon teased. "I'm so scared . . . *not*! Here's some hand-to-hand Pummel Whacking!" Ogremon threw fast punches in Ikkakumon's face almost too quickly to see.

Ikkakumon bellowed in pain. "Harpoon Torpedo!" he yelled, and the horn launched off the top of his head. As it

zoomed toward Ogremon, the horn split open, and a metal rocket sprung out. The rocket buzzed into Ogremon, knocking him into his crate.

"Joe!" Ikkakumon called. "You've got to climb up on my back!"

Joe quickly hopped aboard, and Ikkakumon sailed away to safety.

"Cowards!" Ogremon called, shaking his club. "Come back and fight! I dare you!"

But Ikkakumon ignored him and swam away.

Joe held tightly to Ikkakumon's horn. "Oh, man," he said. "I never wanted adventure. I'm more a stay-home-and-read kind of guy." Then he noticed how weary Ikkakumon looked.

"Really tired," Ikkakumon muttered, his eyelids drooping. "Hungry . . . sinking . . ."

"Sinking is bad," Joe said. "I thought you were supposed to be some sort of super water-mammal!"

Suddenly Ikkakumon shrunk back into Gomamon. Joe was thrown clear, and he plopped into the water.

Joe struggled as he sunk into the depths of the ocean. Gomamon couldn't help him.

He had conked out from exhaustion.

Sora and Biyomon had crash-landed in the water near a broken section of File Island. Though they had easily climbed onto land, Sora's bed still washed up against the rocks with a rhythmic clunking.

As soon as they'd dried off, Sora built a fishing pole with vines and sticks. She cast out into the deepest water around the island.

"Sora is fishing, Sora is fishing," Biyomon sang. She looked like an oversized pink parakeet. "Catch anything?" Biyomon asked.

"Not yet," Sora said. "Give me time. I'm hoping to catch something big."

"I'd even be happy if you caught me a little sardine," Biyomon said.

The stick Sora had used for a bobber suddenly ducked down under the water with a sharp tug.

"Look!" Biyomon exclaimed. "Maybe there's one now!"

"Oh boy," Sora said as she strained against the taut fishing line. "It feels like a whale! This is a whopper for sure!" She clenched her teeth as reeled in her catch.

Biyomon grabbed Sora around the waist. "Let me help!"

The two of them pulled—and a boy's head popped above the surface.

"Help!" he coughed weakly.

"That's a person!" Sora cried. "Joe!" She worked even harder at pulling him to shore.

Sora and Biyomon dragged Joe onto the beach. Gomamon was holding on to Joe's leg.

"Thank you," Gomamon sputtered.

Later that evening, with Joe out cold by a campfire and the stars twinkling overhead, Gomamon told their story.

"Then a large crate drifted over to us," he explained. "Ogremon popped out and attacked us."

"Goodness!" Sora broke in. "How horrible!"

"It was," Gomamon replied, "but I digivolved, and we escaped him. Then my strength left me. The next thing I knew, I was sinking deeper and deeper."

Gomamon paused, staring into the flickering flames. "When I opened my eyes and looked around," he continued, "I finally spotted Joe nearby. He was unconscious at the time and sinking fast. I tried to get him to the surface, but my strength was giving out again and I couldn't hold my breath much longer. That's when your fishing line hit me. So I grabbed it and wrapped it around Joe and hung

on until you pulled us in."

"Oh, my goodness!" Sora exclaimed. "I'm so glad both of you are okay!"

Gomamon lowered his voice. "But I'm worried about Joe," he said.

"Joe's going to be just fine, Gomamon," Sora promised.

Gomamon nodded. "Well, yes, physically," he said, "but I'm worried about his emotions. Fighting Ogremon back

there really knocked him out. He needs to rebuild his self-confidence."

"How can we help him?" Biyomon asked.

"Very simple," Gomamon replied. "We just make him

our leader."

Joe groaned, waking up. He pulled on his glasses and sat up, frightened. "Hey, where's Ogremon?" he demanded. "Huh?"

"He's gone," Biyomon said.

Sora raised her arms dramatically. "But we've got a bigger problem!" she exclaimed. "We can't find the others! What should we do? We're stuck on this deserted island with no leader! So, I guess you'll have to lead us, Joe."

Joe blinked behind his glasses, confused. "What?"

"I'm for him!" Gomamon cheered.

"Not me!" Joe cried. "I'm not a leader!"

"You have to," Sora told him. "You're the strongest one here."

"Not to mention the bravest!" Biyomon put in.

"Remember how you fought Unimon?" Gomamon reminded Joe.

Joe stood up. "I am brave!" he shouted. "I am the

brightest one here!"

"Well, let's not get too carried away," Sora muttered.

Joe let his shoulders slump. "No," he moaned, facing Sora. "If I fail, who will save you or me?"

"My fishing line!" Sora joked.

A faint sound of church bells rang through the night.

Joe tilted his head, listening. "Did you hear anything?"

"Yes," Sora replied. She pointed to the top of a hill, where there was the outline of an old church's steeple. "It

seemed to come from up there," she said.

Joe smiled. "Wherever there's a church, there's usually people," he said. "And maybe our friends!"

The four of them stomped along a path in the woods, climbing up the hill toward the church. Joe called out an army marching chant: "Hut, two, three, oh, your left! Two, three . . . oh, your left! Two, three . . . oh, your left!"

"Must he keep up that army nonsense?" Sora whispered to Biyomon.

On a stone pathway that led to the church, Joe stopped suddenly. "Halt!" he cried. "Notice anything?"

Sora stared at the shadowy churchyard, shuddering as she spotted rows of gravestones. "It all looks sort of familiar to me," she said softly, "as if it's a place I've dreamed about. Or *déjà vu*—you know, like we've been here before."

"Right," Joe replied. "This definitely looks like the island part that broke away. So we should find everyone else taking shelter in that church! Or at least some *other* people."

"You're assuming quite a bit there," Sora put in.

"Fine!" Joe snapped at her. "That's my *opinion*!"

Sora shrugged. "I'm just giving another view."

"I'm the leader here!" Joe shouted.

"Excuse me!" Sora shot back.

Joe turned away from her and strode toward the church. "Let's move out!" he ordered.

As he stormed toward the building, Sora hung back a little with Gomamon and Biyomon. "Wow, we've created a monster," she whispered.

"Hey, you think a Black Gear got him?" Gomamon joked.

"Gomamon!" Sora scolded. But she couldn't help laughing.

"Step lively now, troops," Joe called back. "Let's have no stragglers! There's the church!" He froze on the path that led to the front door. "Oh . . ." he breathed.

"What are you waiting for?" Sora asked Joe.

"Uh . . ." Joe stammered nervously. "Uh . . ."

"C'mon, Joe, you're the leader!" Gomamon said. He sighed, pretending to be out of patience. "Do you want me to take a peek?"

"No, I don't want you taking a peek!" Joe replied. "I

can't *wait* to go in there!" He stomped away, toward the church.

"I think it worked," Gomamon whispered to Sora and Biyomon. All three of them smiled.

Avoiding the front door, Joe crept alongside the building with his back pressed against the wall. He lurked in the shadows as he inched toward the door. "Okay, I'm afraid," he muttered under his breath. But then he gathered his courage and peered around the edge of the door.

Inside, he could see a group of people swaying in a dorky dance, all holding hands.

"I was right!" Joe whispered to himself. "Just a normal group of people!"

He hurried back to the others. "Hey, guys!" he called. "There *are* people in the church, dancing! Badly, I might add."

Sora, Biyomon, and Gomamon all sneaked toward the church to look for themselves. Sora peeked around the door frame. "There *are* people," she said. "They're dancing, and they're wearing masks . . . like it's Halloween!"

Oddly, the masks seemed to be just normal men's and women's faces.

Then a stranger wearing a man's mask appeared next to Sora.

"Hallo-*what*?" he asked.

Sora, Joe, Gomamon, and Biyomon all screamed.

When the kids and the Digimon calmed down, the masked man pushed the door open to let them have a good look inside the church. "They're celebrating the Bakemon holiday," he explained. The man pronounced the name of the holiday *back-a-mon*.

"It is like Halloween!" Joe said excitedly.

"We'd love to have you join us," the masked man said. The dancing had stopped, and another bunch of masked people hung out by the altar. "You arrived just in time for some Bakemon trick-or-treat fun."

"Wait," Gomamon said. "Bakemon . . . as in *Lord* Bakemon?"

"Yes," the man replied again.

Gomamon scratched the side of his head. "But the only Bakemon I know of is a horrible Digimon who lives among ghosts as their ruler!" he exclaimed. "Why would you honor and celebrate someone like that? In the words of our friends, he's a . . . *loser*!"

The masked man stared intensely into Gomamon's face. "Don't you dare come in here telling us who to honor or not!" he hissed.

"You're a little touchy!" Sora told the man. "We just want to know when the trick or treating starts."

"You're not afraid?" the masked man asked.

Sora, Joe, Gomamon, and Biyomon shook their heads.

"Well, you should be!" the man cried. "It's a trick—" His mask shattered, and out sprang a big white ghost with dark black eyes. His mouth was full of sharp shark's teeth. "And you're the treat!"

Joe and Sora screamed as the masked people changed before their eyes.

They were all ghosts, and they all looked very hungry as they swooped through the air toward the kids and the Digimon.

Joe, Sora, Gomamon, and Biyomon bolted for the exit. "This is worse than Halloween!" Joe hollered.

Hunted by the ghosts, the kids and Digimon zoomed into the graveyard. Around the tombstones stood the people who had been dancing earlier.

"I'll bet they're ghosts, too!" Sora screamed.

Sure enough, the dancers yanked off their masks, revealing evil sheet-white faces underneath. "That's right!" the ghosts wailed.

The ghosts quickly surrounded Joe, Sora, Gomamon, and Biyomon, shrieking. The kids howled in terror.

But then Biyomon got serious. "Spiral Twister!" she hollered.

A green swirl of energy spun out from her wings. It

blazed into the ghosts, and knocked five of them down.

Gomamon dashed toward the ghosts. "Gomamon, digivolve to—"

But Gomamon toppled onto his face in the dirt. "I need food," he muttered exhaustedly. "You were right, Joe . . . I should've saved some earlier."

Biyomon flew closer to the remaining ghosts. "Biyomon, digivolve—" she began, but she grabbed her stomach and fell out of the air. "I'm hungry, too," she moaned. "I can't digivolve!"

The ghosts surrounded the kids and the weak Digimon, quickly capturing them.

A bunch of the ghosts dragged Gomamon and Biyomon away from the kids, pulling them into a back room of the church. The ghosts hauled the Digimon over to a small, stinky jail cell.

"Get in there!" one ghost snarled, tossing the Digimon inside.

Gomamon and Biyomon belly-flopped onto the cell floor.

The ghosts laughed as they slammed the bars shut with a loud clang.

For a few minutes after most of the ghosts had left, Biyomon inspected the cell for a possible escape route. She shoved a stone in the wall, but it didn't move. "There must be a way out of here," she said, pacing behind the iron bars.

"Maybe we've been looking in all the wrong places," Gomamon suggested.

Biyomon gestured around the cell with her wing. "There's not much room to look in this place."

A snore echoed off the stone walls. Biyomon and Gomamon peered through the bars at the ghost guarding them. He'd fallen asleep on a wooden crate.

"Hey," Biyomon whispered. "We may be able to trick the guard and escape. But first we have to wake him up."

The dumb ghost snored again, and a snot bubble inflated out of his nose.

"I think I have just the thing," Gomamon said. He

122

picked up a tiny pebble and tossed it at the ghost. It popped his snot bubble.

"Ooh, hey, what's the idea?" the ghost groaned in a brainless voice.

"When do you start?" Gomamon called.

"Start what?" the ghost asked.

"Start taunting us," Gomamon answered, "you big floating bag of wind!"

"But I haven't learned how to taunt anyone yet!" the ghost protested.

"Here's how you taunt," Gomamon instructed. "We're starving. And we want to eat. So you show us food, but don't give it to us. Got it?"

"I think I gotcha!" the ghost replied, nodding stupidly. "You know, I've got a bunch of bananas!"

"So, taunt us with them," Biyomon said, pressing her face up against the bars of the cell. "C'mon!"

"Okay," the ghost said. He pulled a purple banana out of the crate and floated closer with it in his hand. "How's this, huh? Looks good doesn't it?"

"I can't see," Gomamon said. "Come a little closer."

"You bet!" the ghost agreed. "See?"

As soon as the ghost was near enough, Gomamon and Biyomon grabbed his arms. Then they clocked him a good one on the head.

The ghost toppled backward, out cold.

"That was a pretty good idea," Gomamon said.

Biyomon chomped on the banana. "Never get between a Digimon and a meal!" she exclaimed.

15

In the church's main room, Joe and Sora had been tied up on the cold stone altar. The ghosts circled around the platform, waving their transparent arms.

Two ghosts floated above the kids, holding giant shakers of pepper and salt. They shook spices down on Sora and Joe, giggling.

Joe let out a huge sneeze when the pepper hit his nose.

"Uh . . . sir?" Sora asked. "Salt and pepper? You're not really going to eat us, are you?"

"You are a little on the scrawny side," a ghost replied, "but you'd be surprised what the right seasonings can do!"

Sora struggled against the ropes. "What kind of fiend would eat us?" she asked. "We're just kids!"

"We like food, we like to eat," the ghosts chanted. "Munching you both will be a treat!" All the ghosts started circling overhead, holding hands as they whirled. "We're scary ghosts," they sang. "We like to boo!" Swirling faster, they mashed together to form one enormous ghost—Bakemon, the nastiest, meanest ghost of them all!

"Now it's time to chew on you!" Bakemon hollered at the kids. He roared, opening his mouth wide, and Joe and Sora screamed.

That's when the kids' Digimon friends ran into the room.

"Gomamon digivolve to . . . Ikkakumon!"

"Biyomon digivolve to . . . Birdramon!"

The church vibrated as streaks of brilliant digital information whirled above. The huge, walrus-shaped Ikkakumon burst up between the kids and Bakemon, blocking him with his sharp horn.

Biyomon transformed into a fiery phoenix—a bird of flame.

"Your timing couldn't be better!" Joe cheered.

Birdramon freed the kids, burning their ropes off them. Joe and Sora sprang off the altar and dashed out of the church. Once outside, they hid behind tombstones.

They were only alone out there for a second. Bakemon stretched his vast arms and shoved Ikkakumon and Birdramon out into the churchyard.

Ikkakumon climbed to his feet. "Harpoon Torpedo!" he bellowed. A missile surged out of his horn, streaking toward Bakemon.

But Bakemon caught the rocket, and tossed it over the top of the church, where it exploded harmlessly.

"Meteor Wing!" Birdramon screeched. She opened up

her wings and streams of red-hot fire rained down on Bakemon.

Bakemon slapped the flames out of the air.

Behind the tombstone, Joe shook his head in amazement.

"He's putting up a good fight!" Sora said. "Lord Bakemon's tough!"

Joe clenched his fists. "We have to weaken Lord Bakemon, to help our friends beat him!"

"*We?*" Sora demanded. "You're the leader, not me! What makes you think we can beat him?"

Joe sat up straight. "I once saw a show about this Roman physicist," he explained. "He believed that repeat-

130

ing a phrase can make mind win over matter, if you really focus."

"Let's focus on running!" Sora suggested.

"No," Joe replied. "We focus on making Bakemon lose his power."

Sora shrugged. "Well, you're in charge," she said. "Start focusing."

Joe closed his eyes like he was praying. "Bakemon lose your power!" he chanted. "Bakemon lose your power!

Bakemon lose your power!" He popped open his eyes and glared at Sora. "Jump in any time now," he said. "Well, help!"

"Right!" Sora shouted. But then she looked nervous. "I don't know . . ." she muttered. "That is . . . I just didn't, uh . . . Oh!" She pulled off her blue cap, and handed it to Joe. "Take my lucky hat!" Sora offered.

Joe put the hat down and drummed on it with a stick, keeping time with his chant. "Bakemon lose your power!" he shouted. "Bakemon lose your power!"

Bakemon shrank. He looked upset and scared as he got smaller and smaller. "Ooh!" he whimpered.

"Bakemon is getting weaker!" Joe cheered. "I believe it's working!"

With a pitiful wail, Bakemon backed away from Birdramon and Ikkakumon.

But they weren't about to let him go that easily. Ikkakumon shot out another torpedo, and Birdramon let loose with another Meteor Wing attack.

Ikkakumon and Birdramon's blasts smacked into Bakemon. The ghost exploded in a big ball of brilliant flame.

Joe laughed as pieces of Bakemon fluttered down from the sky like tissue paper. "You got beat!" he yelled happily.

"Way to go, guys," Sora told her big Digimon friends. "You got Bakemon!"

Ikkakumon and Birdramon laughed as they sat down for a rest.

Suddenly a jagged crack zigzagged across the grave-yard, splitting the ground open.

"It's an earthquake!" Joe screamed.

Sora remained calm. "But we're not shaking," she

said. She walked over to the crack and peered into its depths.

When she saw what was inside, Sora gasped. "Look!" she cried. "Those are Black Gears!"

Joe hurried over and looked at the dozens of gears turning deep inside the crack. "Lots of them!" he added.

Abruptly, the gears stopped spinning. They began to fall apart, crumbling. The island lurched, and Joe and Sora stumbled, trying to remain standing.

"*Now* we're shaking!" Sora cried.

But the island only vibrated for a moment before it started to sail calmly on the ocean once more.

"I'm glad those Black Gears broke," Joe said.

"And I'm glad Bakemon's gone," Sora put in.

Joe glanced over his shoulder, and spotted the top of a tall peak in the distance. "Look!" he exclaimed.

"It's Infinity Mountain!" Sora cheered.

"Let's go!" Joe shouted. He climbed onto Ikkakumon's back, and the big Digimon plunged off the island, swimming toward the mountain in the distance.

Birdramon picked up Sora and swooped aloft to follow Joe and Ikkakumon in the air.

"Maybe our friends are there!" Joe called to Sora.

"I hope so!" Sora replied. "I really hope so!".

137

Hey, kids! By now you've all probably armor-energized into the exciting second season of Digimon Digital Monsters™. Here are a couple of cool games and puzzles using names you'll see in season two.

HAVE FUN!

R T S E C   F O
_C r e s t_   _o f_

G D W O L E E N K
_K n o w l e d g e_

UNSCRAMBLE
THE PHRASE...
THEN COLOR THE
PICTURE!

word finder

Can you find these digi-words in the puzzle? Look up, down, across, back, and diagonally.

GATOMON   T.K.   JOE   KARI
WORMMON   YOLEI   CREST   MIMI
SHURIMON   SORA   CODY
HAWKMON   TAI   DAVIS

```
S H U R I M O N   O N
H Y Z Z S I V A D   D
A Y W P F T K   R
A W N O M O T A G
K K C R L I K R I
M R M C E M I E
O E M N O I I T
N S O R A D X G
Q T N J O E Y S
```